The Lantern Fox

If you enjoy reading this book,
you might like to try another story
from the **MAMMOTH READ** series:

The Lantern Fox

Garry Kilworth

illustrated by
CHRIS CHAPMAN

mammoth

To Oscar and Henry

G.K.

To Natalie,

with love

C.C.

First published in Great Britain in 1998 by Mammoth
an imprint of Egmont Children's Books Limited
Michelin House, 81 Fulham Road, London SW3 6RB

Text copyright © 1998 Garry Kilworth
Illustrations copyright © 1998 Chris Chapman

The rights of Garry Kilworth and Chris Chapman to be
identified as the author and illustrator of this work
have been asserted by them in accordance with the
Copyright, Designs and Patents Act 1988

ISBN 0 7497 3281 4

10 9 8 7 6 5 4 3 2

A CIP catalogue record for this book is
available from the British Library

Printed in Great Britain by Cox & Wyman Ltd,
Reading, Berkshire

Contents

1 *April meets the fox*

IT WAS LATE autumn with its dark-early evenings. April was walking home in the dusk, following the hedgerow footpath. She had been fishing in the river and carried her rod in her right hand. In her left was a backpack containing her bait box and canvas stool. She enjoyed angling because it allowed her to be on her own.

Though the darkness was sweeping in swiftly, April was not afraid. In fact she liked the dark. She could hide in the dark. April hated attention of any kind. She liked to be unseen.

Suddenly, April stopped. Something had darted into the ditch which ran on the other side of the hedge. It was the size of a smallish dog, perhaps a fox or a badger? But it had not been a dark figure, as it should have been in the twilight. It had glowed with a strange light.

April blinked, wondering if she were seeing things. She did not want to pass the spot where this creature lurked in case

it jumped out at
her. Strangely, though,
she felt quite calm and steady.

'Hi!' she called into the silence of the
night. 'Get out. Go on. Go away.'

The creature remained crouched in the
ditch. April could see the glow of a bright
heart through its coat. Then she heard
another noise from the edge of Hidey

Wood nearby. She could just make out a
man. In the crook of his arm was an open
shotgun. Sitting at his heels, listening

intently, was his dog. It was the local farmer, Mr Polkinghorne. She recognised him by his broad squat outline.

'Don't give me away,' whispered a deep voice. 'Please don't tell them where I am.'

April felt a prickle of fear go down her back. Who was speaking? Surely not the animal in the ditch? But there was no one else around.

'Tell who?' April asked in a tight voice.

'Those two. Farmer and dog. They're out to get me.'

'Why – why do they want you?'

The creature gave a short cold cough, barely loud enough for April to hear, but the dog immediately went up on its haunches, its ears pricked.

Mr Polkinghorne did not notice his dog's alert attitude. He snapped the shot-gun shut, which jerked the dog's attention back to its master. They moved away, walking down into one of the folds in the hills.

A sound like a soft sigh came from the creature in the ditch. 'Have they gone?'

'I think so,' said April. 'Yes – they've left now.'

'Thank goodness.'

April was once more unafraid. It was difficult to be scared of something which spoke in such a reasonable tone of voice. She walked forward. There in the ditch was an animal which shone with an inner light like a lamp in the dark. A thrill of wonder went through her as she knew she was looking down on a very unusual creature.

'Don't come any closer. Stay where you are!'

She stopped. 'Why, what's the matter?'

'I – I'm afraid of you.'

'Afraid of *me*? I won't hurt you.'

'What's that in your hand?'

'This? It's a fishing-rod. It's not a *gun*, if that's what you think.'

'It looks like a whip – but – but if you say it's a fishing-rod, I believe you. You see, I'm a fox. A dog fox. I'm a little chary of whips. Huntsmen carry whips when they lead the foxhounds against me. What's that bag thing? Have you got any dead fish in there?'

'No – anglers like me always put the fish back in the river after they've caught them.'

She thought the fox would be pleased, but he seemed peeved. 'Silly thing to do. I'm hungry. A nice trout would have gone down well.'

The fox emerged from his hiding-place and stood on the path before April. Even in the poor light she could see he was a handsome fellow, if a little thin. His soft inner glow was stronger now. How did he manage to stay so luminous? Where had he learned to speak?

'Why can you talk?' asked April. 'Why do you shine like that?'

The fox growled in the back of his throat.

'Some kind of woodland magic. Who knows? I drank deeply from a pool with a reflection of the moon in the water, but whether that had anything to do with it or not I don't really know. It's bad enough during the day, but look at me now! How can I hunt like this? My prey can see me from a mile off. And the farmer's after me. It's only a matter of time before I'm shot or starve to death.'

'Oh, you poor thing,' said April.

'Well, it's not your problem. I don't know why I'm talking to you like this. I don't like being so close to a human. You smell funny.'

'Well, so do you,' retorted April, stung by this remark. 'You smell like a dog with a damp coat.'

The fox shuddered. 'Don't mention dogs to me. My cousins! Ha!'

April stared at him. He really was a good-looking fox. His coat was reddish-grey in the evening light. His elegant tail swept out behind him. He walked neatly too, with a fine sense of balance. A litheness. There was intelligence behind his amazingly bright eyes.

'What are you going to do now?' she asked the fox.

He did not reply. April watched him for a few moments as he stepped nimbly over the flints and small clods of earth. Then she called out again.

'Wait. Why don't you come home with me. I – I can get you something to eat from the house. I don't think Mum would let you stay in the house. She's terrified of dogs. But you could stay in the potting shed.'

The fox stopped in mid-stride and

turned back again.

'You haven't got any other pets?'

'There's Albert, my brother's guinea-pig, but he's in a cage.'

The fox nodded thoughtfully. 'No cats though? Cats are not chasers but they're quite savage when they want to be. If you surprise one by turning a corner and bumping into it, they get very nasty. Well, go on then.'

April led the way, wondering if she were doing a very foolish thing, but filled also with an exciting sense that something marvellous was happening.

2 *Fox around the house*

THE LIVING-ROOM light in April's cottage beamed a warm welcome through a chink in the curtains. These days April looked forward to going home. It had not always been so, before her parents divorced and her father moved away. She missed the times when her father had been nice to them, but now he had gone it was generally better. The cottage was more peaceful.

'You go inside the potting shed,' said

April. 'I'll go and find you something to eat.'

The fox sniffed the air nervously. 'There's a German shepherd dog on the loose. I can smell him on the night wind.'

'That would be Sabre, Mrs Arkright's dog, from the cottage down the lane. She lets it roam around a bit. It doesn't hurt anyone.'

The fox shivered. 'It would go for me, all right.'

April tried to think what to do next.

The potting shed was choc-a-bloc with garden tools and the lawnmower. There was no room for the fox. She would have to sneak him into her bedroom.

'I read a story once where a Spartan boy in Ancient Greece hid a fox inside his

tunic,' she said, looking down, first at her light anorak, then at the rather large animal by her side, 'but you look too big for that.'

There was a clatter of dishes from inside the cottage.

'Hmmm, Mum's in the kitchen. Look, we'll go in, I'll get her attention, and you nip into the bathroom. I'll come for you afterwards.'

April opened the front door with her key and then pointed to the bathroom at the end of the hall. He trotted off obediently.

April went through to the kitchen. Her mother looked up. 'April, you know I don't like you out alone after dark, even if it is only half-past four.'

'Sorry, Mum – lost track of the time.'

'Well, make sure you keep track of it in future. Come in before dark, not after-wards.' Her voice softened. 'Any luck with the fishing?'

'Didn't catch anything.'

'Never mind, dear. Perhaps next time. Would you scrape the carrots, please, while I do the potatoes. Listen, I bumped into Mrs Ludgate on the way home from work.'

April inwardly groaned. Mrs Ludgate was one of her school teachers.

'She says you're quite bright, but . . .'

April knew what was coming.

'. . . she says you don't put yourself forward enough. She says she's sure you know the answers to some of the questions she asks the class, but you don't offer to reply.'

'I don't like people looking at me.'

Her mother sighed. 'I know, dear, I

used to be shy myself – but you seem to want to crawl into a dark corner somewhere.'

'Mum, can we change the subject, please?' April pleaded.

Her mother sighed again and shook her head sadly. 'All right, dear. Now, go and wash your hands and call Tim from his bedroom. I don't know what that screen thing's doing to that boy's eyes . . .'

To April's horror, as she left the kitchen she saw her younger brother coming out of the bathroom.

'What were you doing in there?' she gasped without thinking.

Tim looked indignant. 'What's it to you?'

'Sorry. You – you just made me jump.'

'By coming out of the bathroom?' grumbled Tim. 'Next time I'll ask permission.'

April ignored him and swept past into the bathroom locking the door behind her. She stared around at the washbasin, the bath, the toilet pan and finally her eyes rested on the door to the airing cupboard where the hot-water tank warmed clean pillowslips, sheets and towels. It was open by a fraction of a centimetre. She grasped the handle and gave it a pull. It refused to open.

'Are you holding it shut?' she whispered. 'It's me, April.'

The door swung open slowly. The fox had been gripping the catch on the other

side with his teeth. He stared up at her. 'That boy smelled of rodent. I had to hide when he came in.'

'My brother,' she said. 'Come on out of there. You'll leave red hairs all over my mother's towels. And you must promise me one thing. You mustn't eat Albert. My brother's very fond of him.'

'I'll try not to.'

April checked that the coast was clear and herded the fox into her bedroom.

'You hide under the bed,' she said. 'I've got to go and eat dinner, but I'll come back afterwards with some food. Are you sure you're all right?'

'Still a bit nervous,' replied the fox, 'but I'm getting used to it. And, April . . .'

'Yes?'

He poked his head out from under the bed. 'I hate human odours, but it smells

better than I expected it to in here. Nice scents. Like spring.'

'It's my Flowers of the Field spray,' she replied, pleased that the fox liked it. She usually did not like compliments. They were almost as difficult to handle as insults or teasing.

April went into the dining-room to find they had a visitor, Bill Patterson. He worked with her mother. He was coming to dinner more frequently lately. April did not dislike him, but her shyness made her suddenly hunch her shoulders. She felt a flutter of panic when he looked towards her and she knew that she would have to speak to him. She tried to make herself as small as possible. Surprise visitors always made her want to run back to her bedroom.

'I don't feel hungry,' she said to her mother, avoiding Bill's eyes. 'Can I go and read?'

'I don't bite,' said Bill kindly.

'You sit down at the table, young lady,' said her mother. 'I can't have you running off and hiding every time we have a guest to dinner.'

Tim thankfully took the attention away from April by saying to Bill, 'Have you played a computer game called "Witches and Warlocks"?'

'No. How about you show it to me after dinner?'

'All right.'

April sat at the table and stared at her plate, hoping Bill would ignore her. Her mother placed a dish of mashed potatoes and carrots on the table. They were a Quaker family so they began their meal with a minute or two's silence. Just as the silence finished and Tim was reaching for the dishes in the centre of the table, there was a faint clatter from somewhere in the house.

'What was that?' asked April's mother. 'Did you hear something?'

April began to panic. 'I didn't hear anything.'

'I did,' said Bill, getting to his feet. 'I think it was in one of the bedrooms.'

'Oh – oh, I know,' cried April quickly, 'it's probably Albert rattling his cage. Mr Patterson, you work with Mum, don't you? What do you do? Are you her boss?'

April's mother looked astonished. It was the first time April had ever spoken to Bill, let alone taken an interest in who he was or what he did at work. Her mouth dropped open, the strange noise forgotten.

Bill, too, was a little surprised, having been defeated by April's shyness so often in the past.

'Me? Your mum's boss? Other way round, April. I joined the firm after her. I'm still only a Grade Two. Your mum's a Section Head.'

'Cool,' murmured Tim, nodding at his mother. 'Boss lady.'

April thought she heard another faint sound from her bedroom and hastily spoke up again. 'Oh, that's – that's interesting. So you're new round here, Mr Patterson? I thought you'd been living near here a long time.'

'Bill – call me Bill.

No, I moved here last Easter. Didn't get to know your mum until about July. Listen, she told me you're interested in fishing. I do a bit myself, when I've got the time. We could all go. You, your mum and me – even Tim if he wants to.'

Tim's screwed-up face showed what he thought of this idea.

Bill added, 'There's a place I go for perch. Perch aren't everyone's idea of a good fish but . . .'

He continued to talk, while Tim shovelled down his dinner and April pretended to be thoroughly interested. He was not really boring, but April would rather his attention was not solely on her. She tried to think what to say to stop him from talking to her.

'And herring, now they're a good freshwater fish,' Bill was saying, smiling at her in a funny kind of way.

'What?' she said, frowning. '*Herring*?'

His smile grew broader. 'I thought you weren't really listening. Anyway, if you all want to come some time, just let me know.'

After the meal she helped her mother wash up while Bill played computer games with Tim. Somehow Tim always managed to get out of washing up when Bill was a guest.

While her mother was clearing the table, with a quick look at the doorway to make sure she was alone, April swiftly opened the freezer. She took out the first thing she saw: a leg of lamb. Her heart was racing. She had never stolen before

and it made her feel terrible, but she could not let the fox go hungry. She hid the meat behind the bread bin under a tea towel. Later she smuggled it, and a half loaf of bread, into her bedroom.

'What was that noise?' she whispered, closing the door behind her. 'You nearly gave the game away.'

'I got bored,' said the fox, shamefaced. 'I was chasing a spider.'

'Well in future you must keep quiet. If Mum finds you here she'll have a blue fit.'

'What colour fit?'

'Never mind,' said April, smiling to herself. 'Look, I've brought you some food.'

She placed a magazine open on the floor so that the fox did not make too much of a mess. He tried gnawing the leg of lamb but it was frozen solid. He worried it like a ball around the floor, trying to get a grip on the icy block with his teeth, banging into chair legs and bed legs. April's heart was in her mouth every time he knocked a piece of furniture. Finally he gave up and ate the bread, leaving the meat for the following morning.

'You sleep here,' said April, pointing to the floor by her bed.

'I might be a bit restless. I usually hunt at night. The smell of that Albert next door is driving me crazy. And it's a three-quarter moon. I like hunting under a moonglow. I like to stalk.'

'You leave Albert alone. Tonight you'll have to hunt in your dreams. Now, no more talking or we'll be heard. Try to sleep.'

April lay awake for a while with the day's adventures running through her mind. She felt quite proud of herself for talking to Bill. She would never have done it if it were not for the fox making a noise. It was strange how he had appeared out of nowhere. He was a spell-binding creature, that was certain. His presence in her room seemed to give it an air of enchantment. In the stillness she could hear the soft, rhythmic thumping of the fox's heart. It sounded like the

far, distant beating of a drum. April imagined a fairy drum might sound like that. It sent soft vibrations through the room, conjuring a wonderful fantastical other world.

'Will we always be friends?' April asked him, hopefully. 'Could you stay here for ever?'

'Stay here? You mean like a pet? I don't think I could be a pet. But I think we'll always be friends.'

'Are you a real fox?' she whispered into the darkness. 'Or are you magical?'

'Ah.' His reply sounded like the rustle of dry autumn leaves in the wind. 'We'll never know that, will we?'

3 *An unexpected visitor*

THERE WERE STILL several days of the half-term holiday left. Normally April would have gone fishing at the lake, peacefully waiting for evening to come round. Today, she had a fox to look after. She also had Polly to avoid. Polly was their cleaner-cum-child-minder, who arrived half an hour before her mother left the house.

Polly said at breakfast, 'You're looking very full of yourself today, miss. Won the lottery, have we?'

'No – it's just – such a nice day, Polly.'

She left Polly with raised eyebrows and returned to her room.

When the fox came out from under the bed, April remarked on the dimness of his light. 'It's definitely not as bright as it was last night,' she said. 'Perhaps it's fading a little now? If it's fading maybe we can make it go faster somehow? What about giving you something dark to drink? My mum's tea is dark brown. My aunt says you can stand a spoon up in it.'

'I tried drinking muddy water, but it didn't help.'

'Wait a minute, you said it began when

you drank from a pool with the moon's reflection in it. It was a full moon a few days ago. Perhaps your light will dim as the moon disappears?'

'It's daylight,' grumbled the fox. 'It always looks dimmer in daylight.'

'But if it *is* fading a little, perhaps one day you'll be back to normal again?'

'One can but hope.' But he sounded a little forlorn.

At that moment there came a tap on the door and Tim's voice called, 'Who are you talking to?'

A surge of panic rose in April's chest. 'No one.'

Then her mother called, 'What's the matter, Tim?'

'April's talking to someone.'

'Nonsense – it's probably her radio.'

'It was *her* voice,' insisted Tim.

April heard her mother's footsteps coming along the hall. She quickly opened the door, to find the pair of them staring at her.

'I – I was practising,' she told them. 'I'm – I'm thinking of going in for the school play. We're doing a shortened version of William Shakespeare's *A Midsummer Night's Dream*. I – I'd like to be one of the fairies.'

They stared at her as if she had just told them she was going to climb up to the roof of the house and jump off.

'The – school – play,' faltered her mother. 'You?'

April lifted her chin. 'Why not? I'm as good as anyone else.'

'But you won't even speak up in class, let alone go on the stage in front of the whole school.'

'I might do,' April said, her stomach churning a little. 'I – I just might do. We'll have to wait and see, won't we?'

With that, April closed her door and put her finger to her lips to stop the fox from saying anything further.

Her mother went to work at nine o'clock and shortly afterwards some friends called for Tim. When Polly went out to the village shop April and the fox were left alone for a short time.

'I'm terrified of people,' said April.
'My dad used to shout at everyone all the
time and I just wanted to make myself invisible.'

'I'm afraid of people too,' replied the
fox, 'but I suppose being a fox that's

natural. I'm scared of dogs, of course – especially a pack of them. Foxes don't like groups of anything really. We like to melt into the countryside, be invisible amongst the woodland trees. That's how we survive, by using our camouflage, not letting anyone see us.'

'I used to pretend I was a fairy who could make myself invisible. That's how I survive . . .'

Here was a friend who understood how she felt about crowded places and being noticed.

'Do animals talk to each other?' asked April. 'I mean, without magic? It would be great if they did.'

'In a way, but not always through

sounds – sometimes it's just the way they move, or sit or change their expressions.'

April decided this was true. Her aunt Mary's cats, Oliver and Henry, sat or sprawled and stared at you with their mysterious eyes, and you knew exactly what they thought of you and your kind.

After showing the fox all over the house, April left him to his meal and got on with some homework.

Luckily Polly had to leave early that day, and the pair of them were able to sit in front of the living-room fire.

At four-thirty, not long after Polly had gone home, there was a ring from the front doorbell. A woman of around sixty

stood on the doorstep. She stared at April through thick-lensed glasses.

'Hello,' she said, peering hard, 'you must be April. You remember me? I'm Mrs Caitlin, one of your mother's Quaker friends. Clerk of the Meeting, actually. Is your mother in? She's expecting me.'

'At work,' whispered April, recognising the lady but trying to hide in the shadows of the doorway. 'Not here.'

'Oh dear,' said Mrs Caitlin, inspecting her watch. 'I'm early, then.'

April now remembered her mother had said Mrs Caitlin was calling later in the day. She did not want to appear rude and finally overcame her shyness.

'You'd better come in, Mrs Caitlin,' she

said quietly. 'Please could you wait in the living-room?'

'Thank you, my dear. Which door is it?' she asked, squinting.

'First one on the right.'

Mrs Caitlin opened the door and walked into the room. April suddenly remembered the fox.

She had left him asleep on the rug in front of the living-room fire!

4 *The sound of the hunt*

APRIL ENTERED THE living-room with her heart in her mouth.

The scene that met her eyes was astonishing.

The fox was sitting bolt upright on a small table. Mrs Caitlin was sitting on the settee, adjusting her coat. Incredibly she was taking no notice of the fox. April stifled a nervous laugh as Mrs Caitlin took off her coat and began to look around the room.

'What a nice picture,' she said as April stood rooted to the spot. 'The one over the fireplace. Devon, isn't it?'

April glanced quickly at the scene of cliffs, sea and flying wild ducks.

'Cornwall, actually – would – would you like a cup of tea?'

'That would be nice,' replied Mrs Caitlin. 'No sugar, thank you. I don't like killer whites.'

April wondered whether Mrs Caitlin was talking about sharks. 'Beg pardon?'

'Killer whites. White sugar, white bread, white – everything. Bad for you, you know. Bad for the digestion and bad for the heart.'

'Oh, then perhaps you'd like to make

your own cup of tea?' said April desperately. 'I'm sure you know the way you like it. I'm not much good at it. I'll show you where the things are in the kitchen . . .'

'Oh, no.' Mrs Caitlin smiled. 'I trust you to do a good job. You're a big girl, aren't you? I can't rummage around in another woman's kitchen. It wouldn't be right . . .'

Her roaming eyes fell on the fox. He sat still as a brick, staring glassily ahead of him. He glowed like a beacon. April thought that at any moment Mrs Caitlin was going to let out a blood-curdling scream and jump up and run. She winced in anticipation.

Instead, Mrs Caitlin peered at the fox and said, 'What an unusual lamp.'

Relief flooded through April. Her visitor was obviously very short-sighted.

'Yes – yes it is, isn't it? We bought it at

a car boot sale.'

Mrs Caitlin looked puzzled.

'It doesn't have a switch or a lead.'

'Batteries,' replied April, quickly. 'It works on batteries. You lift its tail to switch it on. Clever, isn't it?'

Mrs Caitlin's hand went out towards the tail.

April jumped forward. 'It's a bit delicate – we've got to get it fixed – I wouldn't if I were you.'

'Oh, sorry, dear,' she replied pleasantly, withdrawing her hand. 'It's just *so* unusual.'

Two things happened at once. There was the hollow sound of a hunting horn. A fox hunt was coming home. The fox's eyes widened in fright. He slipped quietly off the table and under the settee. Fortunately there was also the sound of a key in the lock of the front door. Mrs Caitlin turned to see April's mother come in.

'Oh – Mrs Caitlin.'

'I came a bit early, but your daughter

here has been very kind. Such an atten-
tive hostess. She would have made me a
cup of tea but we got talking. You must be
very proud of her – a girl of her age with
the confidence to entertain a grown-up!'

'Why, yes I am,' replied April's mother
faintly. 'Thank you, April.'

'That's all right, Mum.' Suddenly, for
the first time ever, April felt very grown
up. 'Oh, and by the way, I've been thinking about getting a Saturday job,' she
said. 'They want someone down at the
farm to help muck out the stables. Is that
OK, Mum? I'll talk to you about it later,
shall I?'

Mrs Caitlin and April's mum discussed their business. When she got up to leave, Mrs Caitlin said, 'I do admire your lamp.'

'Lamp?'

'This – oh dear, it seems to have disappeared. It was an animal lamp. A dog, I think. With batteries. Here, on this table. Did April take it with her? I didn't see. But then my eyesight isn't what it was. She said it needed repairing. The tail switch was broken.'

April's mum stuttered out some confused reply as she led Mrs Caitlin to the front door and let her out. Some moments later she came into April's room.

'Mrs Caitlin spoke about some sort of dog lamp by the settee. Do you know what that's all about?'

'No, Mum, unless it was one of Tim's toys. Probably one of his transformers. Gogamagog, the robot truck from Mars or something that changes into a dinosaur. He lights up. It's probably fallen down beside the settee. I'll go and look for it.'

April immediately went to the living-room and looked under the settee. The fox stared out at her. His teeth were white and glistening. If he had not been an animal she could have sworn he was grinning at her. She felt like laughing herself and this time not from nervousness.

'Yes, here it is,' called April, as her mother went to the kitchen to begin making dinner. 'I'll put it in Tim's room.'

'Thank you, dear. And thank you for looking after Mrs Caitlin.'

'Pleasure, Mum.' Again, that feeling of having fulfilled something special went through April.

The fox drifted out of the living-room, along the hall. He paused by Tim's bed-

room with its open door and cast a
longing glance towards Albert. The
guinea-pig was furiously rearranging his
straw bed. Albert looked up and blinked
at the monstrous carnivore in the doorway, then seemed to realise he was safe
behind bars and continued to attack his
bed. The fox sighed and slipped into

April's room.

Later, at dinner, Tim was told off.

'Stop leaving your toys all over the place. You nearly gave Mrs Caitlin a funny turn today.'

'Who, me?' exclaimed an indignant Tim. 'I never.'

'You always say never, but they seem to find their way into every corner of the house, just the same, young man. There's no need to look so aggrieved. Just keep them tidy in future. Your sister's been tidying up after you. You should thank her.'

Tim glared daggers at April, who smiled sweetly back at him.

'I never,' he grumbled quietly, to get in

the last word, but there the matter was allowed to drop.

Once more April had managed to keep the fox a secret.

5 *An empty freezer*

OVER THE NEXT few days April
managed to keep the fox from
human view. She had to put herself forward a lot, to draw attention away from
her room or wherever the fox might be
hiding. It was becoming easier.

The fox's inner light was beginning to
fade, day by day. Whatever it was that
glowed inside him was starting to wear
off as the moon itself waned in the
evening sky. Perhaps she would have to

release him back into the wild, but she did not want to think about that too much. She wished she could keep him for ever, but he had already said this was not possible.

The freezer was emptying fast. As April took sausages and other meat from the back she built a wall of frozen peas and other vegetables in the front to hide the emptiness. What would her mother say when she found most of the meat gone?

One day the fox told her, 'I'm not used to being trapped by four walls. It's like a prison to me. I feel like an Albert. All my life I lived in the open air. The only time I've been inside a place like this is when I got into a chicken coop.'

'I don't want to hear about that,' said April quickly. 'All right then, I'll smuggle you outside today. We'll go into Hidey Wood and you can have a run.'

'Sounds reasonable,' the fox said. 'How do we do it?'

April took down her backpack.

'You'll have to go in here. I'll pretend I'm going fishing.'

The fox climbed inside the canvas bag reluctantly. It took all his will not to scream like a banshee, in the way foxes sometimes do. As it was, he twittered like a frightened bird. April warned him he must stop. Then she took up her fishing-rod and went through the cottage to the front door.

'Just going fishing!' she yelled. 'Be gone a couple of hours.'

She carried the heavy bag to the wood at the end of the footpath which ran outside the cottage. There, safe inside the trees, she opened the bag and the fox jumped out. He sniffed the air joyously.

'Listen to the earth,' he murmured. 'It sings with a thousand different scents.'

She watched him race through the wood, sending up showers of red, yellow and gold leaves. His nose was drinking in the odours all the time. His sense of smell was his strongest survival weapon, better than his sight, which was really quite poor. Better even than his excellent hearing.

He was such a nimble creature too: much more like a cat than a dog. He could balance deftly on a thin branch of a tree. With one single flip of his rear end, he could turn in full flight and be racing in the opposite direction.

The colour of his coat changed in different lights: one moment he was grey like a wolf in shadow, the next he stood rust-coloured like a red squirrel caught in a shaft of light. His eyes were bright and eager-looking. A slim red tongue showed its tip between his pure white teeth, as he concentrated on his athletic movements. What struck April most of all was his ability to remain completely silent as he wove in and out of trees like a downhill skier, quiet as a ghost.

'You really are a beautiful creature,' she told him.

'I know,' he replied immodestly.

After another quick joyous run, the fox

said something to April which upset her,
though she had been expecting it.

'I shall leave you in two days' time.'

'Why?' she said, her heart sinking. 'You – you don't have to . . .'

'My work is done.'

'What do you mean, your work?'

'We've helped each other. You know what I mean.'

And, thinking about how her confidence had grown, she believed she did.

Suddenly the fox smelled man on the wind. He jumped back into the bag just as April heard the crunch of footsteps on dry leaves and twigs. She turned to see Bill coming towards her. She shrank inside herself.

'You shouldn't be out here in the woods on your own,' he said, concerned. 'I thought you'd be down by the lake with the rest of the anglers.'

'I was – I was just going,' she mumbled.

Bill nodded, but he was staring at the backpack.

'What's in there?' he asked. 'I thought I saw it move.'

April considered telling a fib, but she thought if Bill really had seen the bag move he would not believe her.

'It's a fox,' she replied, her chin defiantly up now. 'But I don't want you to see it.'

He regarded her for a while with a blank expression. Then he shrugged.

'Fair enough. If you say there's a fox in there, I believe you. I don't understand what you're doing with a live wild creature

in a backpack. It seems a bit cruel to me,
but I trust you have good reason, April.'

'Thank you. I do have. I do.'

'Your mother sent me to look for you. She said there's a lot of meat missing from the freezer. I thought I'd warn you so that you can think about what you're going to say to her.'

Back in the cottage April's mother was livid.

'You took all that frozen meat? April, what for? What on earth did you do with it?'

'I fed it to a fox.'

'What?' exclaimed her astonished mother. 'Why did you do that?'

'The same reason as you feed the birds. I feed the foxes.'

'But meat is expensive, April. I was going to make a stew tonight. Bill came

round specially.'

'I'll go to the supermarket and get some more,' said Bill. 'It really doesn't matter.'

'Mum,' said April, 'I had to do it. I'll pay you back. I'm getting that Saturday job soon, at the farm. I'm sorry I've made you unhappy . . .'

'You haven't made me *unhappy*, April. I just don't understand you. I didn't realise you felt so strongly about wild creatures. You don't have to buy any more meat, but please ask in future. If you want to feed wild animals I'll get you some scrag-end from the butcher.'

'I want to pay it back, Mum.'

Bill said quietly, 'I shouldn't interfere, but why not let April pay it back if she wants to. It obviously means something to her.'

'All right,' said her mother, throwing up her hands, 'pay me back – but leave my freezer alone in future. All that meat!

I don't know. You two aren't having a joke with me, are you? Is this a conspiracy?'

'No joke, Mum. I'm sorry. I wish it was.'

'Well, I don't know. Bill, would you mind? Going out to the supermarket, I mean? All I've got are potatoes and carrots.'

'Be happy to. Car's still warm outside. Back in a jiffy.'

When he returned he had some extra minced steak in his pocket which he gave to April secretly.

6 *Back to the wild*

TWO DAYS LATER the fox's light had faded completely and it was time to go back to his beloved outdoors.

'I know you feel sadder than I do,' said the fox, his voice sounding faint and weak, 'but we animals are not as sentimental as humans.'

It was almost winter. April wondered how he was going to survive in the wild, with ice and snow locking the land. She was appalled at the lean times which lay ahead of him. In a few weeks his stomach would be in a tight knot of hunger. She wanted to bring him food, but he refused.

'I can manage on my own. I shall miss Albert though. There's always been the delicious scent of a small snack next door.'

'That's not very nice. Into the bag, Mr Fox!'

April smuggled the fox out of the house for the last time.

Tim, seeing her backpack, said, 'Don't you get bored, sis? You never catch anything.'

'I like to be out of doors. You're happy in front of your PC. I'm happy sitting on the grass with a rod in my hands.'

April called to Polly on her way out. 'Be back in a few hours. If anyone wants me I'll be down by the lake, near the old oak. I've got to make up my mind whether I want to be in the school play or not. I'll have to audition for the part I want next week, if I'm going to do it at all.'

Polly shook her head slowly and smiled.

'There's been such a change in you lately, young lady.'

April carried the fox all the way to his earth, under the roots of an oak. It was quite cleverly disguised by the roots, but around and about the oak were bits of bone and scraps of fur and various other debris.

'I'm not very tidy,' explained the fox, his voice fading. 'None of us foxes is.'

'Perhaps – perhaps I can come and see you sometimes? Shall I come back here, to your earth?'

'Soon I will not recognise my young friend. It is better we say goodbye now.'

'If we have to. Goodbye.'

'And thank you,' he said in a faraway voice. 'Some part of my fox spirit will always remember you, even if my mind does not. We shall remain friends for ever, even if we do not see each other. It was not an accident that we met.'

Then racing over the landscape he went, his magnificent red tail riffled by the wind. He shimmered, like moonbeams in windblown trees, and mysteriously was gone. April blinked, wondering whether she had seen him slink swiftly into some bushes, or whether he had vanished before her eyes. All that was left of him was the faint scent of his coat which mingled with the smell of fallen damp leaves.

April went home that evening after sitting by the lake for most of the day, not fishing exactly, but simply staring at the water and the scene around her. She still loved fishing, but no longer because it was a solitary sport. In fact, she was looking forward to going back to school. It was quite exciting to wonder if she would make some firm friends. She felt as

if she had been freed from a prison, let
out into the open air, to walk, to run —
even to fly.

Six weeks after the fox had gone back to
the wild, April's mother went to an open
evening at the school.

'She's much more sociable than she used to be,' said her teacher, 'and she's auditioned for the school play and got a small part. That's astonishing, considering how terribly shy she used to be.'

'Yes,' replied her mother proudly. 'It's as if she has an inner glow of confidence now. She's started a Saturday job at the farm near us as well . . .'

When April went to bed the night before the performance, she was feeling some of those old familiar twinges of panic.

She woke to find the full moon shining through a chink in the curtains, and heard the distant voice of a friend barking in the cold darkness. It was a comforting sound. His spirit was calling to her one last time. It was telling her she would be all right.

It made her think about how he was getting through the winter.

Foxes lived such difficult and hazardous lives. Foxes did the unlikely. *Magical* foxes did the impossible.

She smiled and said to herself, 'All I've got to do is pretend to be fairy Cobweb in front of some friendly parents. *I* can do the impossible too!'

If you enjoyed this
MAMMOTH READ try:

Lionheart

Lynne Markham
Illustrated by *Chris Chapman*

There is a special lion in
Grandad's study. It's dead, but
when Leo touches its mane, golden
sparks snap and fizz . . . and Leo
is transported to the African veldt.
He becomes the lion.

Leo is convinced that his
grandfather and great-grandfather
share this bond, but why did his
great-grandfather kill the lion?
Each time the spirit of
the lion takes him over, Leo comes
closer to uncovering the mystery
of the dead lion . . .
and the truth about himself –
ROAR!